The Call of the Wolf

Carmel Reilly   Christina Miesen

Nelson Thornes

Nelson Thornes

First published in 2007 by Cengage Learning Australia
www.cengage.com.au

This edition published under the imprint of Nelson Thornes Ltd,
Delta Place, 27 Bath Road, Cheltenham, United Kingdom, GL53 7TH

10 9 8 7 6 5 4 3 2
11 10 09 08

The Call of the Wolf
ISBN 978-1-4085-0091-0

Story by Carmel Reilly
Illustrations by Christina Miesen
Edited by Johanna Rohan
Designed by Heather McDonald
Series Design by James Lowe
Production Controller Hanako Smith
Audio recordings by Juliet Hill, Picture Start
Spoken by Matthew King and Abbe Holmes
Printed in China by 1010 Printing International Ltd

Website www.nelsonthornes.com

The Call of the Wolf

Carmel Reilly   Christina Miesen

Contents

Chapter 1

Hearing the Call

Ruki opened his eyes
and stared into the darkness.
He had heard something.
He lay still and listened.

Then he heard it again.
A sound like a howl.

"The call of the wolf,"
he said slowly,
and shivered.

Ruki had been waiting to hear
that call for almost a year now.
But, even so, he was afraid.

He knew that he would have
to go out to meet that wolf.
He knew that it would be
one of the most important things
he would ever do.

Ruki got up and went outside.
He saw his father standing
by the fire,
warming his hands.

He looked at Ruki.
"Did you hear the call?" he asked.

Ruki nodded.

"Then you know it's time
to go to the cave in the woods,"
said his father.
"You will be alone there
for many days.
It will be a big test for you."

Chapter 2

The Cave

Ruki started to shiver again
as they walked into the woods.
His father took his hand and said,
"Don't be afraid if the wolf comes.
You will know what to do."

At the cave, Ruki's father gave him
a bag of food, a knife
and some sticks for a fire.

Then, he said goodbye and left Ruki
alone in the cold and the dark.

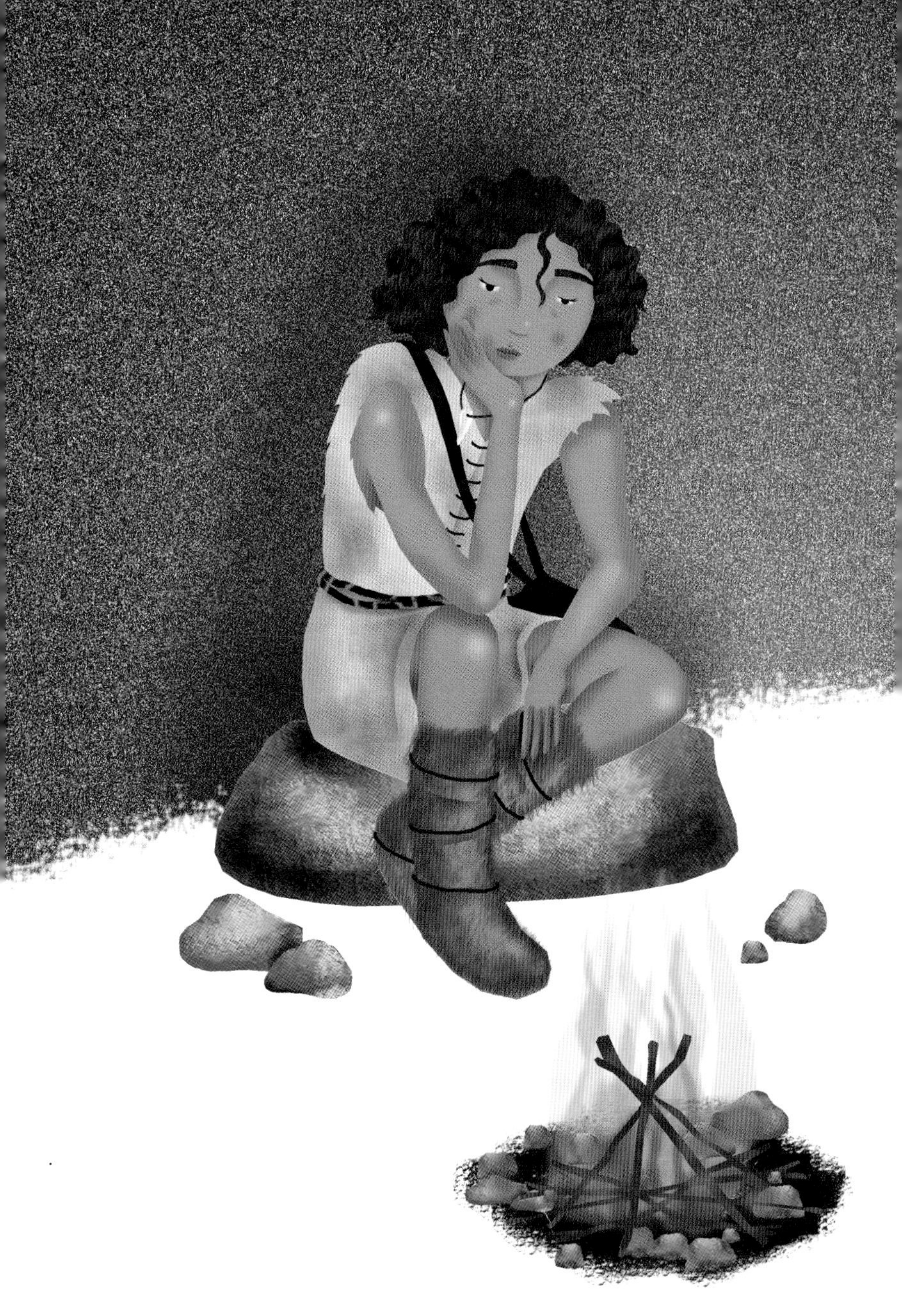

Ruki made a small fire.
He sat down and stared into it.
He began thinking about
what he would do
when the wolf came.

Over the next few days,
he didn't sleep much,
and he didn't eat at all.

Ruki heard the wolf's call
at night time.
The cave was so dark
that Ruki could not see past
his small fire.
But, he knew the wolf
was not far away.

He grabbed his knife and waited.

Ruki could feel the wolf was closer.
As he stared into the dark,
he heard a low growl.

"Wolf?" he asked quietly.

Slowly, Ruki reached down
and put his hand into his bag.

Chapter 3

Ruki Faces the Wolf

Ruki pulled out some food
and used the knife to cut it up.
Then, he began to throw
some of it into the darkness.

"I know you're hungry, wolf.
Please come and take the food,"
he said.

Suddenly, the wolf came out
of the shadows,
just behind the fire.
Without looking at Ruki,
it bent over the food
and began to gulp it down.

Ruki kept throwing the wolf more food until, at last, there was none left.

When the food was gone,
the wolf looked up at Ruki.

Ruki stayed very still.
"That's all I have," he said quietly.

Ruki could see the wolf staring at him, and he stared back.
Then, the wolf turned and left.

The next day, Ruki walked back
to his family.
He felt good.
He had met the wolf.
He had passed the test.